The Four Seasons of Her

of

Her

A fictional poetry novella by S. A. Duncan

Table of Contents

Preface...5

Prologue..7

Introduction... 11

SUMMER 14

FALL 45

WINTER 76

SPRING.. 108

Afterword 140

Epilogue 142

Preface

Dedicated.

To those who have loved.

Lost.

And loved again.

Because love.

Her sweet, delicate nectar.

Drizzling down the back of your throat.

So that even if the aftertaste turns bitter.

One can never forget her luscious ambrosia's climax.

As she whispers: 'Always a pleasure.

Till I see you again.'

Prologue

This is written for.

Me.

Her.

You.

Woman.

For each season that we've endured and conquered,

without the praise we so richly deserved.

This book.

is one of our untold tales.

Clothed in opiate-swaddled poems.

Perhaps,

to mask the stench of regret and shame.

Its' dull bones carefully stacked beneath the crotchet doilies

in the forgotten cupboard.

Hidden purposely by the special porcelain china,

now rotted and dry.

But still locked away.

Until such a time.

As today.

As now.

So that together,

we could weather this 'In between place;'

The rugged road from | **where our love first started,**

to where it broke | .

For we all are twined by the same emotions.

No matter how much we hide.

Nothing stays buried.

It just grows more on the inside.

Maturing with the trauma,

and worse, still corrupting our pride.

So, dust off these potpourri-scented skeletons;

no longer bleached and white.

Run away the bony spiders,

taking advantage of your plight.

Stare at your afflictions;

the ones scarring your left side.

And fight.

Fight fiercely against it!

For we can bend.

But do not have to stay broken.

We can love.

Fully.

Time and time again.

But we must remain open,

to **Love**.

For it is our home.

Do you hear me?

This is our home too.

I just hope you believe me.

This book is largely a work of fiction.

Cover design by: Sean Jn -Francois .
Painting by: Venny George.

Location: Saint Lucia x USA

This isn't your typical poetry.

This isn't a regular book.

Just a spill of <u>love</u> and <u>loss</u> through seasons.

If you're daring, take a look.....

Introduction

Welcome to the Four Seasons.

Over here, we are unconventional.
Letting you, our guests be the ruler of your mental journey.

We will transport you through the intricate layers of time.
If you let us, that is.
But you must submit,
to yourself,
and to us.
We will reach deep within,
to uncover all what needs to be found.

So, grab some wine to unwind,
while we unravel the deepest layers of your mind.
Just close your eyes,
and sink deeper this time.
To activate your journey,
a chance of a lifetime.
To experience the past,
and recourse in real time.
Each season unraveled.
It starts with a ripple,
a draw.
a toss on a dime.

SUMMER

The place where it all began.

Sonnet I

Summer was.

Soothing.

At first.

The serene salty breezes of the ocean at dawn,

sun kissed by the sun's timid rays.

Watching a fleet of fishermen and their boats slow dancing across the waves.

Accented by the noisy wails of tenacious, hungry sea gulls in flight,

as they towered over the sea and caves.

I sink my bare feet further through the coarse, white sands.

Nature's energy pulsating beneath my toes,

as I move to the beat of her drum.

Floating to her hypnotic sound.

And yet such a peaceful rhythm.

Tranquil.

Home.

Sonnet II

Summer was.

Warm.

Like the subtle streams of sunshine glimmering through the window blinds,

as the rooster crows diligently to start the morn.

Followed by the synchronous barks of startled, sleepy dogs,

as the familiar voice of 'Juke Bois' creeps hastily with the 6 a.m. alarm.

Blaring incessantly,

but still such an intimate, cultural routine for many.

And yet,

I am nestled by the warm aromas of mom's cooking:

Warm bakes, salt fish and cocoa tea.

My favorite.

Strong island spices teasingly pervading my nostrils.

Nudging me from slumber.

A slow seduction.

Perfect entrapment.

| **Juke Bois** | : Well-known radio journalist Sam 'Juke Bois' Flood known for his morning radio show spoken in the Saint Lucian native dialect (Kweyol).

| **bakes** | : a popular Caribbean breakfast item which is usually fried, soft and doughy and made with flour. Normally served at breakfast time with sautéed salt fish & cucumber salad in Saint Lucia or also with cheese, butter, jam or jelly.

| **salt fish** | : dried and salted fish, usually cod from the Northern Atlantic that is usually stewed or sautéed for a variety of traditional Caribbean dishes.

| **cocoa tea** | : Traditional chocolate tea made with roasted and ground cacao nibs, milk and warming spices (such as nutmeg and cinnamon).

Sonnet III

Summer was.

Pleasurable.

The satisfaction of sweet pulp oozing around the corners of my mouth,

after raiding my neighbor's famous Julie mango tree.

Finding refuge on his hammock,

as it rocked back and forth to the melodious tempo of rustling leaves.

And the tiny echoes of tropical birds chirping near and far.

Swarms of kaleidoscopic butterflies fluttering through his flower pots,

while my brothers wrestled for ripe guavas and plums in the nearby trees.

Transfixed in that blissful moment.

Smooth, eclectic nostalgia.

| **mango Julie** | : One of the many varieties of mango species that is grafted. Julie was recognized for its outstanding flavor: rich, tangy, fleshy yet non-fibrous and its small dwarf growth habit as it is a very compact dwarf tree.

Sonnet IV

Summer was.

Gratifying.

Joyous, booming laughter amongst childhood friends.

Sitting outside of our trucks on one of our famous round-de-islands.

Listening to 'dennery soca' as we whine rhythmically,

amidst vibrant libations and rotating mary janes.

Floating through cloud 9.

An inebriating flush of energies dissipating through a cerebral time lapse machine.

Reminiscing about moments, old and new.

That back to the future type de ja vu.

Sweet, organic euphoria.

|**Round-de-island**|: A day long road trip along the coast of the island where individuals stop at each place of interest or historical landmark to eat, drink and have fun.

|**dennery soca**|: A new, upcoming and extremely popular raw adaptation of SOCA music consisting of Kuduro music, wild drums and suggestive lyrics using the native St. Lucian language 'Kweyol'/Creole. The Dennery segment was named after the town it was birthed in, 'Mabouya Valley, Dennery' in St. Lucia. Some local artists include: Subance, Freezy, Mighty, Big Sea, Mata and Migos, Black boy, Krome, Nassis, etc.

Sonnet V

Summer was.

Enchanting.

Skin tight bikinis and copper sunset tan lines.

Shaded by swaying palm trees,

as I sip on the refreshing lushness of coconut water.

Watching the tide drift in to embrace the shoreline.

A delicate french kiss foaming white with each caress.

Her shells; fallen stars of the sea on the virgin sands,

as she beckons me in.

So, I obey.

Submerging myself beneath her crystal-clear waters with ease.

So temperate.

So peaceful.

My air bubbles rising quickly to the briny surface.

Such gentle protest from my lungs.

Yet I am unmoved in this moment.

Tiny fish nibbling at my toes,

as green seaweed dangle against my feet like slippery anklets.

Surrendering completely to the will of the ocean.

An Entrancing,

Ephemeral,

Dreamscape.

Sonnet VI

Summer was.

Feverishly exhilarating.

The type of 'Fever' only Vybz Kartel could unleash through song.

The music pulsating through my bones as it infuses into my very being.

A harmonious beat that entices my subconscious into full submission.

So, I dance.

A slow, intimate love affair

between a soul and a sweet melody.

Pure vibes.

|**Vybz Kartel**| : One of dancehall's most successful musical artists from the island of Jamaica. He released the single "**Fever**" from the album 'King of the Dancehall' in 2016 which topped both local and international music charts.

Sonnet VII

And then summer became.
Him.
His eyes; the brightest almond brown,
Staring straight into mine.
A merriment of sparks harnessing before us,
spreading like wildfire.
And now our worlds collide.
Running around naked by the river side.
Playfully incanting desires upon potent moonlight.
Perpetual conversations dripping from all tongues,
as his words stretch over the silk of my velvet,
like the neon dust fluttering from the moon's chest.
His airy fingerprint anchoring gently beneath my rib cage,
with each warming breath of him that I inhale.
Slowly...
Deeply...
Till I am giddy.
Souls both spilled,
and now wholly drunk,
on each other.
Surrounded by nothing but trees
from the countryside.
Oh such charming bliss,
for a Lucian version of Bonnie x Clyde.

Sonnet VIII

Summer was.

A tale

of the predator and the prey.

An enticing chase laced with slow, bated, sadistic torture.

My appetite growing as his pheromones lured me into his artifice.

Till I am paralyzed.

Engulfed by his juices like a Venus Fly trap.

His sap transporting me through a cannibalistic erotic flight.

As I lay in his tormented flower bed.

He devours me;

Stealthily,

Ravenously,

Completely.

Sonnet IX

Summer was.

A movie.

A crimson eruption of broken suns descending at the horizon.

With exploding gold silhouettes in full masquerade.

And yet,

I was focused on his shadow as it melted into the darkness.

And still,

I remembered his red-hot lava consuming the quivering
depths of my mound.

A scorching love affair that could make a volcano jealous.

A supernova explosion.

Of his son setting into my sunset,

whilst the sun was setting where the sea and sky met.

Sizzling.

Sonnet X

Summer was.

Him.

And the heat.

For it was intimidatingly and unbearably humid amidst clear, blue skies.

But the air was thicker with the aroma of our lovemaking,

as I rode his throbbing width in the backseat of his 2009 Ferrari 458 Italia.

Sweating glorious sin as we glide across the leather seats.

Stifling throaty remnants of the oral alphabet,

till we are both spent and saturated.

Marinating in our selfish desires.

Cinematic fleeting pleasures.

Sonnet XI

Summer was.

Our first carnival.

Surrounded by the joyous screams of excited parading masqueraders playing mas.

As we glide in our multicolored costumes drizzled in exuberant feathers and glistening jewels.

Serenaded by the ultimate soca tunes from Machel and Ricky T blaring through the speakers.

And I immerse myself fully in the bacchanal.

Pure euphoria.

He grabs my hand and steals a kiss from my alcohol stained lips.

The sweetest discord.

Thrusting me firmly into the boughs of his hips,

as we gyrate slowly and seductively.

Till we are lost in each other.

Totally in sync.

Even in a crowd.

Even if only for a moment.

Time had simply stood still.

|**Carnival**|: One of the most significant events on the islands' cultural and tourism calendar where islanders wear costumes in different bands for a street parade usually lasting two or more days.

|**Soca music**|: Genre of Caribbean music originating from Trinidad and Tobago.

|**Mas**|: shortened word for masquerade. The crafting of costumes or the act of being in costume or parading in a carnival.

|**Machel Montano**|: Famous and successful Trinidadian soca singer known for his high energy and fast paced songs and performances.

|**Ricky T**|: Famous and successful Saint Lucian soca singer known for his witty lyrics and infectious bangers.

<u>Sonnet XII</u>

Summer was.

Full.

Of hazy, intoxicating nights.

Tugging at the moon as her sweet lustrous elixir dissipates into the milk of my supple breasts.

Fueling our warmest desires into raging beasts of the night.

The quickening of tempered bodies combusting into panted breaths and steamy nights.

His aroused rod parting my pink lips like the red sea,

as he thrusts intently into the softness of my thighs.

Till climax.

A plethora of quivering orgasms.

Moonlight has always been my aphrodisiac.

And him; my addiction.

The perfect menage-a-trois.

Sonnet XIII

Summer was.

Me.

Chasing Waterfalls.

With friends that became family.

Energies unmatched.

Conversations transcending the rifts of space and time.

While we float on clouds of freshly rolled reefer.

Spitting magical haikus through sense heightened portals,

as the sound of water cascading below coos us to a
temporary hypnosis.

And we drift....

Further and further.

Till our minds rise,

To meet the pregnant wake of the sunrise...

|**Chasing waterfalls**| : A tour available in St. Lucia by tour guide and soca artiste Casim James [Amazona Adventures] which takes you deep into the island to the most beautiful, untouched and remote waterfalls.

Sonnet XIV

Summer was.

Wild.

Of dreams where he could quench the tillness pervading my senses.

Of his eyes undressing every pink petal anchored inside my satiny blossom.

Growling hungrily,

he parts my legs as his smoldering heat rises.

It was a slow desirable thirst.

Only quenched by my honey as it liquified on the curves of his mouth.

Like fervent red Moscato.

Chilled.

Flowing.

As he sips.

Longingly.

Voraciously.

Drunk off my fountain of desire.

I am awoken by the radiating heat of his pliant iron pressing against my back.

Rigid and pulsing;

Only to be neutralized by the flood swelling up in my stimulated core.

His body shuddering with each plunge as my walls clench tightly around his steel.

Stifling unanimous moans to his warm seed bursting into my softness.

Such tempestuous delights.

Raw.

Wildly delicious.

Fantasy meets reality.

Sonnet XV

Summer was.

Soon to end.

And suddenly the days felt like minutes.

And the hours; seconds.

Time; a passive reminder of my happiness

And yet an active reflection of my gloom.

A premonition perhaps.

For the magic came and left.

Before we ever could.

Pink linings fading on silvery clouds

As we part,

a lover from her muse.

And that was.

Summer's faithful end.

Now we enter

FALL

where it started to go left.

Sonnet I

Fall was.

A dragon.

Spewing fiery red pastels over everything in its path.

Stripping all life of everything summer.

Evergreen trees obliterating into flaming orange-yellow hues.

As golden butterflies illuminated in the rays of the sun.

It was a beautiful sight.

A masterpiece.

A slow waltz between nature and nurture.

Ushering in the crisper air of October.

Sonnet II

Fall was.

A bountiful harvest.

Bursting with pride.

Of rosy apple blossoms parading their scarlet gowns.

Pumpkins overgrowing their sturdy vines,

and piles of ripened pecans and chestnuts plumping heartily
for warm, homemade pies.

All embellished with autumn's rust colored leaves.

Twirling to a harmonious lullaby.

Euthanizing all flora to a peaceful sleep.

A tale forced by nature.

Sonnet III

Fall was.

A stairway.

A fluid transition from our summery nights to blissful autumn mornings.

He was the muse to my every thought.

His ink dripping all over me.

Drenching my poetry with his prose.

"Be mine!" he whispered nibbling against the tenderness of my chest.

Stifling a moan, I chucked lightly.

For he didn't know that I was already his to have.

In every capacity,

I was unequivocally his.

Tragic.

Sonnet IV

Fall was.

Effervescent.

For the moon was full of new love.

And every phase of her was drenched in our lust.

Insatiable appetites nipping at our buds.

Generating waves that even oceans thrashed in envy,

as he pounded stealthily against my shorelines.

And the moon glimmered with anecdotes of our sultry
fantasies.

To disappear at first light with our secrets so suckled,

that not even the sun dare uncover.

Such a sweet torment.

For a habitual lover.

Sonnet V

Fall was.

Thanksgiving.

The orchard's treasures harvested and cooked to perfection.

To accent the old faithful turkey with cranberry sauce and my
favorite stuffing.

To dine among family and friends.

And to eat to the heart's content.

A charming persuasion to mend all mistakes,

and be thankful for blessings.

But the more I think about today,

the more I miss home more than anything.

Time has a funny way of showing us,

that our home is our everything.

Homesick abroad.

Sonnet VI

Fall was.

Fierce.

He was a ferocious wolf, and I; his temptress.

Under a crescent moon, we basked in her radiance.

She was bewitching in every right.

And he transformed in the wake of her magic.

Imprinting his ardent desires with each thrust into my core.

Slow steady strokes.

Howling enchantingly to our simultaneous descent.

His animalistic hunt now tempered through the warmth in my eyes.

As we lay breathless and spent in the evaporating twilight.

A girl and her wolf.

Sonnet VII

Fall was.

Torrid.

Of monsoon rains

On the greyest of mornings.

Raindrops pattering on the window sill.

And the chillness creeping through the air.

Sending goosebumps down my vertebra.

Nuzzling onto my neck,

he rips my nightgown away.

Tracing soft kisses along my fevered skin,

till his tongue hungrily drains the juices from my succulent mound.

Pure ecstasy.

I moan louder,

and louder.

Rhythmically;

to an upbeat crescendo of pleasure.

Drowned by the tears of the sky.

As his phallus pounds into me.

Harder

and harder.

Till our euphoric descent.

Sonnet VIII

Fall was.

Him.

Broken and troubled.

And yet he only found solace in the spread of my thighs.

Crumbling beneath my touch as I stroked his ego.

His pride was a lion;

Proud, dark and menacing.

And now it was wounded.

The world was never a forgiving place.

And its bite was far colder than its bark.

So here in my arms,

he needed to heal through my essence.

I licked his every bruise

in my self-made safe-haven.

Even alphas feel broken inside,

and are consumed by self-loathing.

Sometimes our men lack the power to hide,

what their hearts have been feeling.

Sonnet IX

Fall was.

A quest.

High on Life,

Love,

and Hope.

He wanted this.

Us.

And so did I.

Fooled by his whispers of a future despite the distance.

Bamboozled by his obsession to be the only one.

My only one.

Although our responsibilities kept us apart for weeks on end.

Perplexing, right?

Yet,

I am giddied by his milk warming my womb.

Like hot pumpkin cider after a long day.

The perfect climax on every tongue.

A worthwhile distraction,

For a girl who was already sprung.

| **sprung** | : slang term for being whipped or so infatuated with someone that it feels like love.

Sonnet X

Fall was.

A revelation.

Yellow drifts of leaves whirling to the operas of gold finches
across a sun burned sky.

As my inhibitions dangled to the ground.

He made it so easy.

Lulling me into arms.

Enthralling me with his mystery.

So, I skated right into my very next fall.

Funny thing about love.

It doesn't hurt till it's over,

and plummeting to the ground.

Gravity's one hell of a bitch.

Sonnet XI

Fall was.

Me.

Realizing that his candle no longer burned for me.

For his wick flickered less with each passing day.

Its embers dwindling like the muted shell of man that I was left with.

And his presence;

just a shadow,

leaving wispy plumes of acrid black, smoke where my heart was.

And yet, I stayed lit for us both.

Continuously.

After all,

I was always strong enough to carry.

But now this man I sustained would turn cold and betray me.

Finding comfort in someone else,

who could not stand a light to me.

Such a fool to believe that life could be just to me.

Feelings came at a price,

and he was indebted to me.

A woman burned out.

Now scorned.

Sonnet XII

Fall was.

A domino effect.

Of a slow and gradual drift between lovers.

That stood Mount Gimie deep.

How foolish I was.

Scared of a mountain of doubt that already stood there.

Letting his words carry weight,

when his actions were abundantly clear.

I could no longer hide

from the truth that I bare.

I had to get off this train,

destined to nowhere.

Plot twist.

| **Mount Gimie** | : the tallest mountain (3145 feet/959 meters) in Saint Lucia.

Sonnet XIII

Fall was.

A masquerade.

Surrounded by people wearing costumes on Halloween night.

Witches cackling, goblins grunting and ghosts boo-ing.

And yet tonight I am crying myself to a troubled sleep.

Missing him or the person I made him out to be.

Held prisoner in my mind to nightmares that would not leave me be.

Realizing that the monsters in our lives are not always under our bed,

or who we make them out to be.

Sometimes they are masked with perfect faces,

vampires walking around free.

Sometimes draining all our love and strength,

just before they flee.

Trick or treat?

Sonnet XIV

Fall was.

Me.

Reminiscent.

Of his mesmerizing smile behind my lens,

or the twinkle in his eyes sparkling like precious gems.

The subtle loss for words,

when it was time for me to go.

It meant 'I miss you baby. Please don't go.'

But what were words anyway,

to a girl who was hurting?

Here I am missing him right now,

on a solitary brooding.

Waiting for his love to return,

like the sun every evening.

The irony.

Sonnet XV

Fall was.

Soon to end.

The fragrant air drizzled with rotting pumpkins and the pungent aroma of compost.

The meadows stifling beneath canopies of roasted copper leaves.

Fanned by the brisk north winds as it creeped stealthily towards the warm air.

It was a hostile takeover.

A shock for everyone still stuck in summer's hangover.

This movie was about to take a twisted turn for the worst.

Fall was almost over.

And sealed with Judas' kiss,

Winter trembled from her slumber.

She was about to show us all the depth of her power.

Next, we bring you

WINTER

The place where all was lost.

Sonnet I

Winter was.

A shock.

For even the most beautiful flowers withered into nothingness.

No longer supple with girth.

Its aromatics stifled by the gusts on a frosty morn.

Dew nipping at her floral jacket,

till she is naked and barren.

For winter was the grim reaper of everything fragile.

But I was always too strong to ever be considered weak.

I was a survivor.

I just had to adjust my feet.

Sonnet II

Winter was.

Hazy.

Searching for answers at the bottom of shot glasses.

Anything to escape his hold.

See, everything reminded me of him.

The incandescent moonlight seeping over frozen lakes,

for many a night, we lay under her silvery watch settling fires
till the day's break.

The nostalgia seeping in from fleets of freshly fallen snow,

like the first time he anchored into me with caribbean sands
below.

The slow scalding fireplace after retreating from the harsh
cold,

much like his veined shaft massaging my throat till his body
explodes.

I even searched for him in love songs,

making him relevant in places he didn't belong.

Seeking refuge under a drunken veil.

And I'm almost too far gone,

to escape or prevail.

I am.

A girl crying ice drops.

Drowning.

Drunk.

Sonnet III

Winter was.

An illusion.

For he was the glass menagerie in my life.

Something beautiful should never have hurt this much.

But the more I searched for him,

the more I cried pearly shards.

My heart had driven me blindly before,

but this one was bad.

I was dying to piece fragments of a man,

and it was making me sad.

But a mirror could have told me,

it was simply driving me mad.

Crazy in love.

Sonnet IV

Winter was.

Me.

Praying desperately.

Urgently.

To be in his arms again.

Love was supposed to defy everything.

Atleast that I remember.

Sometimes despite time and sickness,

like 'A walk to remember.'

But who am I kidding?

Romantic movies were just a man-made fantasy.

And I, a lover of love

A hopeless tragedy.

|**A Walk to Remember**|: Inspired film by Nicholas Sparks about two teenagers who fall in love with each other despite the disparity of their personalities and one of them having cancer.

Sonnet V

Winter was.

Me.

Waiting for him to come back to me.

To say, 'I'm sorry.'

For everything.

But the seconds felt like hours.

And the hours; days.

That's the thing about time.

She was a trickster with flair

Fooling us,

as she dragged on in our moments of despair.

Ice queen.

Sonnet VI

Winter was.

The coldest.

To date.

A blizzard of heightening regrets and forlonging.

For sometimes accepting the lies just to keep him from leaving.

A self-inflicted pneumonia.

Staining a soul far from deserving.

Naïve of me to believe that everyone was worth saving.

Especially the ones whose emotions were fleeting.

He loves me, He loves me not.....

I count with each brooding.

But the truth of it all,

I already knew the answer I was hunting.

Perhaps the trees felt it too,

as they stood tired and moping.

We were both naked in a storm,

and our bodies were just coping.

Sonnet VII

Winter was.
My excuse.
I blamed her cold, horrid ice fortress for my pain.
And her crystalline dew, the tears I wore as a chain.
I had fallen.
I was broken,
crumbling under his weight.
Trying my hardest to stay sane,
and not to succumb to my hate.
Not even loneliness or hurt,
could drive me into the arms of another.
I realized no one else could fix this void,
he was the only buffer.
Such tainted love for a man was making me sadder.
Sometimes we break our own hearts,
Sometimes we make ourselves suffer.
Heartbroken Anonymous.

<u>Sonnet VIII</u>

Winter was.

Accepting.

That enough was far more,

than enough could restore.

| For heartache never shares fair.

To what you can bare |.

A shipwreck.

Sonnet IX

Winter was.

A much needed island Christmas.

Speckled with countless lights, dashing reindeer and aesthetic inflatable snowmen.

Bon fires outside crackling below roasted pigs.

Overflowing with infectious laughter of drunkened friends, family and foes.

As we drink chairman's spiced rum,

and the kids; ginger beer.

Watching my grandmother tiptoe inside,

to spike the sorrel for more cheer.

But nothing beats the scent of cloved ham sizzling in the oven.

Or maybe trying to open presents before the brink of morning.

Such a perfect distraction from everything else that was brewing.

Thankful to God even more for the joy of his season.

Enjoying Saint Lucia.

And family was the reason.

| **sorrel** | : a festive drink made from dried calyces of the sorrel flower and steeped in boiling water with ginger and whole spices such as all spice, cinnamon sticks and cloves.

| **chairman's spiced rum** | : popular St. Lucian rum infused with local spices.

| **ginger beer** | : fermented alcoholic beverage made from sugar, ginger and ginger culture.

Sonnet X

Winter was.

That faithful New Year's Eve

And a frigid snowstorm.

Exploiting repressed emotions and severe longing.

That even when he begged to see me,

it was mostly my desires that chanced the encounter.

For our lust always burned far brighter than the heat
emanating from his chevy.

So I knew what this was;

nothing more than the physical.

And that was enough for me.

I straddled him desperately, riding his staff.

Windows fogging up as I brace firmly against it.

Our handprints all over the stained glass.

And we become lost in this moment.

His screams deepening with each thrust.

Convulsing until he finally melts into my core.

Hunger sated,

as I melt into him.

Temporary insanity.

Sonnet XI

Winter was.

Me.

Letting it hurt.

Letting me break.

So I could heal.

A hopeless romantic,

damned to a non-romantic world.

A warm-hearted sphinx,

Trying to survive the blistering cold.

A gypsy deep in love,

with a man who was fool's gold.

Seeking closure from impossible things.

That much was true.

I now had to find myself.

To get to my breakthrough.

Mischief managed.

Sonnet XII

Winter was.
Most of all.
A teacher.
Proving that there was life,
even after love was stricken and buried.
Leaving behind a tombstone of my former self,
I was done lamenting.
It was too cold to wait,
too cold to beg for a savior.
Sometimes we have to be our own hero,
despite the time or weather.
Sometimes we must push the boulders off,
to be as light as a feather.
Weightless.

<u>Sonnet XIII</u>

Winter was.

Me.

Realizing three seasons in,

that he was **not** meant for me.

| **And the last time my heart broke**,

will not be the last time | .

Even if I promised myself it would be.

The last time.

The last time ago.

Sonnet XIV

Winter became.

Quite a few things.

But not him.

For it was irrevocably cold amidst blankets of never-ending snow.

Her icy grasp tightening a noose around my neck,

as I shivered with her emptiness.

Like the hollow space that he boroughed deep within me;

with a resulting numbness that encircled the delicate layers of my heart.

But with time,

I felt the change shift within the marrow of my bones.

No longer subtle,

but bounded just as earnestly as the hands on the clock each second.

That's the thing about seasons;

we expect that they change,

but get hurt when people do too.

Not knowing that in life,

The only constant that stays constant is the | **constant change in you** | .

<u>Sonnet XV</u>

Winter was.
Almost over.
The snow started to melt,
and so did the ice around my heart.
Coincidence.
I think not.
Everything had to begin again.
Exactly where it ended.
Everything
and everyone.

Finally, we say hello to

SPRING

Its' no longer the Inbetween.

Sonnet I

Spring was.

Lush.

Like the Garden of Eden.

The earth breathing its first sign of life.

Abundant with multicolored blooming flowers in every waking sight.

Bees bustling through meadows,

and birds taking flight.

Each singing a merry tune,

of God's faithful might.

Winter's tears dissolving,

thanks to the sun's bursting light.

The grass was finally greener

No longer in an icy blight.

Sonnet II

Spring was.
Making him immortal through my pen.
But now thoughts of him,
are no longer thoughts of him.
Love had a way of making lifetimes out of moments.
And I guess heartbreak did too.

Sonnet III

Spring was.
A release.
Escaping from my self-induced prison.
No longer caged by hurt or insecurity,
or weak from his poison.
We women tend to blame ourselves,
guilt ridden by our pity.
But the truth is,
sometimes we get hurt,
not because we are guilty.
Sometimes,
we are too good at fixing,
and loving,
and living.
Sometimes,
we attract hurt men,
because they also need saving.
But.
|I am no longer nursing souls|.

Sonnet IV

Spring was.
My rebirth.
A phoenix emerging from dying embers,
of a past life,
and rotten Decembers.
But now,
I am rising,
burning
unleashing.
Robed fully in strength,
courage and understanding.
Ascending on wings,
that soar even when standing.
I am a fiery flame,
hell bent on surviving.
Ashes to ashes.
Dust to his heart.

Sonnet V

Spring was.
A revelation.
Only time can tell if it was truly love.
And looking back on this year,
it may not have been the above.
Love does not hurt,
abuse,
or live in doubt.
A lesson to be learned fully after my first drought.
Now I am manifesting in my oasis,
with lingering sweet perfume.
Skin fluorescing under moonlight,
delicate feminine rituals to my womb.
It was summer in Springtime.
There was a joy in my soul.
This was my dominion.
Living a story untold.
Call me Sahara.

Sonnet VI

Spring was.
April's 1st.
After months of not answering his calls,
or texts.
Safe to say feeling nothing for him,
was better than feeling anything at all.
We all cope differently I guess,
healing from a fall.
Took him months to notice my well was dry,
I no longer drowned in alcohol.
I moved on without apologies.
I grew from a cement wall.
You'd be surprised what we can reap with no closure,
or when we refuse to be someone's rag doll.
My silence was his blessing.
My heart standing tall.
The jokes were now on him.
April's fool
| **blocked** | .

Sonnet VII

Spring was.
A peace of mind.
A tranquility that could not be bought or bargained for.
With each passing moment,
planting seeds of positive lore.
Blossoming flowers in my mind.
Reciting continuous mantras,
of all the things I adore:
"I am strong,
I am intelligent,
I am beautiful,
And kind.
I am worthy,
I am loving,
I am enough,
I must stay on my grind."
You reap what you sow,
and I was sowing mine
Repeating and believing,
what the stars already aligned.
Destined for greatness.
My future was mine.

Sonnet VIII

Spring was.

Easter.

An awakening.

Ebullient symphonies of Christ's resurrection.

Celebrated by believers worldwide in the most exuberant
fashion.

First church with our palm leaves,

to show respect for his passion.

Then kids chasing bunnies,

lighting up colored factions.

In search of chocolate eggs,

hidden hot on their trail.

All dazzled in bright colors,

To march the specially adorned veils.

Signifying a new life for us all,

a brand-new day.

God's sacrifice to us,

to light up our way.

Sonnet IX

Spring was.
Moving on.
And that was a reckoning.
Staring at new prey gawking in the distance.
His mouth watering at the thought
of my honey oozing all over his tongue.
And I, pacifying the overwhelming desire to hunt,
to devour.
And so I wait.
Releasing my trap,
a single calculated
thread
The wind caressing my silken strands,
till it delicately settles and kisses the breadth of his oak tree.
For weeks I've delayed this encounter.
Carefully studying him,
craving him,
building my appetite for him.
But now it was time to hunt,
time to eat.
Danger,
It was time to feast!
Love trap from a black widow.

<u>Sonnet X</u>

Spring was.
A toast.
To the new me.
Outrunning seasons had taken its toll.
And after months,
finally,
I had beaten the cold.
I no longer woke up scared,
anxious,
or controlled.
I was thriving and blooming,
a huge weight off my soul.
Such a beautiful disaster.
Each day was pure bliss.
I was laughing and dancing,
in my newly found abyss.
| **Girl on that no fuck boy glow** |.

Sonnet XI

Spring was
A tornado.
A sensual storm casually brewing inside,
and with each breath, a deep yearning took over.
He was the sweetest distraction for my momentary pleasure.
And now I wanted desperately to gift him my treasure.
The feeling was succulent and exhilarating.
And I was chastised by it all.
Like a spinning whirlpool of air flirting with my ego's beckon
call.
I was a seductress,
capable of bringing men to their knees.
While I garnished their face with my cream,
all for a tease.
And he was no different.
That much was clear.
I'd devour the air he breathed,
with little or none to spare.
Till he is breathless,
and panting.
Kneeling at my throne.
And only then,
when he begged for it,
I'd release my cyclone.
A mermaid and her siren song.

Sonnet XII

Spring was.

Surprisingly chilly today.

My breath, an icy cold kiss for such a springtime morning.

A foreign sharp welcome to the warmth in his piercing brown
eyes.

He undressed my flimsy gown as I lay before him,

His eyes; as mesmerizing as his nobility.

And as he savored the citrus and honey scents etched in skin,

deep within this paradise,

he felt the wake of a shivery island.

Taunting him with every frosty glimmer that he tasted.

However, he was relentless in his pursuit,

And I in turn,

enjoyed his curiosity as it trickled down the arch of my spine.

He was as hot as a furnace.

And I eventually unraveled before him.

A deserving intoxication for a worthy opponent,

That much was certain.

I was cold as ice,

but with his touch,

I melted.

Sonnet XIII

Spring was.

The world.

Waiting.

To find his fingerprints between the cages of my heart.

To find his kisses underneath the cobwebs of my soul.

To find his love caressing the tip of my every tongue.

To find his scent drizzled onto the caramel stitching of my skin.

While our nights are laden with laughter, cuddles and sweet memories.

And our mornings in bed,

greeted by his warm breaths,

nestled by dawn's light.

And him; as lost in me,

as much as I am lost in him.

Stuck in an abyss where our galaxies collide.

Sonnets about a man with nothing to hide.

|**Love welcome**|.

Sonnet XIV

Spring was.

Me.

On Spring break.

Dressed in fluorescent glittered bikinis soaking up the warmth,

surrounded by raging teenagers all hyped up for the fun.

Drinking till moonlight until the liquor is done.

Vibing to EDM,

shimmering like the sun.

Dancing with glowsticks,

getting shot by waterguns.

Getting kissed by strangers,

Flashing our buns.

Living life to the fullest,

because we only have one.

A girl in Ecstasy.

Sonnet XV

Spring was.
A rejuvenation.
The perfect ending of the four seasons.
She was an effortless flow of nature,
as she coos us a sweet lullaby.
Sweetening by the hour.
Aromatic perfumes of new life in every flower.
Lilies, cherry blossoms, orchids, tulips and daffodils.
All bathed lovingly in dew's shower.
Canary birds on elegant wings fluttering through the air.
Sweet treasures at rainbows end,
to grace her Sunday wear.
Hypnotized by her beauty,
Flora; a spirit of magical flair.
An enchantress on shimmery wings,
confetti in her hair.
As she chants:
"Flower child
Flower's mild
Sweet fairy child
Sweet fairy's wild
Be mine
And stay for a while."
And so I did.
A hippie in wanderlust.
An end to a new beginning.

Farewell for now.

|The New Seasons are Approaching|.

Afterword

Thank you for joining us at the Four Seasons.
We hope that your time here lived up to the fuss.
We pray that each season,
whichever you're in.
Will bring you some comfort,
and restore all your loss.
I bid you farewell now,
moving on is a must.
We do not live in the past here,
in the present we trust.
Let your moments from now on,
Be radiant as star dust.
May your love runneth over,
As you live and adjust.
| **Always a pleasure.**
Till we meet again. |

Dear Reader,

Enjoyed reading **The Four Seasons of Her**? Can't wait for part II: **The Four Seasons of Him**?

Let me know by leaving an honest review of the book where it was downloaded.

And turn to the next page to see what's in store....

Thank you for reading,

S. A. Duncan.

Epilogue

[From: **The Four Seasons of Him**]

Can a rose smell as sweet?

Like the honey suckle and vanilla scents dripping through her

tresses.

Her wit; the softest thorns adorning her voluptuous caramel skin.

Her mouth; puckered with honey drenched lips,

Dripping warm sonnets of love with her every word.

Her voice; nothing more delectable than the way she

moaned,

Delicate whimpers embellishing the orgasmic tingles

cascading through her satin flower.

Her essence; so thick that even the air becomes heavy with

her poise and grace.

For she grew best in the wild, but her buds still bloomed as the

most delicate,

succulent yet soft to the touch.

But her scent? Hmmm..

Her fragrance was aromatic even in dawn's dew.

She possessed the perfumed tartness of about one hundred

ambrosial flower blossoms.

And yet you ask...

Can a rose smell as sweet?

Among roses?

Quite possibly.

As her?

Impossibly.

See, she was simply impossible to forget.

He knew that.

And now his world was full of regrets.

Oh, such wonderful irony.

At a time that her love is nothing more than some bittersweet

poetry.

Made in the USA
Middletown, DE
25 August 2019